Dragon Trouble

Penelope Lively

Illustrated by
VALERIE LITTLEWOOD

BARRON'S

New York • Toronto

First edition for the United States and Canada published 1989
by Barron's Educational Series, Inc.

First published 1984, reprinted 1985, 1988 by
William Heinemann, Ltd, Michelin House, 81 Fulham Road,
London SW3 6RB

Text © Penelope Lively 1984
Illustrations © Valerie Littlewood 1984

All rights reserved.
No part of this book may be reproduced in any form, by
photostat, microfilm xerography, or any other means, or
incorporated into any information retrieval system electronic
or mechanical, without the written permission of the copyright
owner.

All inquiries should be addressed to:
Barron's Educational Series, Inc.
250 Wireless Boulevard

Hauppauge, NY 11788

International Standard Book No. 0-8120-6136-5

Library of Congress Catalog Card No. 89-358

Library of Congress Cataloging-in-Publication Data
Lively, Penelope, 1933-
    Dragon trouble/Penelope Lively; illustrated by Valerie
    Littlewood.
        p.   cm.
    "First edition for the United States and Canada"—T.p.
verso.
    Reprint. Originally published: London: Heinemann, 1984.
    Summary: Peter's birthday gift to his grandfather two
strange looking eggs begins a series of adventures when the
eggs hatch into dragons.
    ISBN 0-8120-6136-5
    [1. Dragons—Fiction.] I. Littlewood, Valerie, Ill. II. Title.
    PZ7.L7397Dq   1989
[E]—dc19   89-358
                                                 CIP
                                                 AC

PRINTED IN HONG KONG
901   9903   987654321

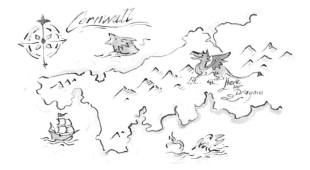

THERE WERE DRAGONS in Cornwall, England once. Hundreds of years ago. Or maybe thousands. It could be that there still are, from time to time—just the odd one, here and there. Anyway, this is what happened to a boy of nine called Peter, last summer.

He was spending the summer with his grandfather, in a small town somewhere around the middle of Cornwall. It was an ordinary little gray stone town with houses and shops and a market

square—not the sort of place where you'd expect to find unusual things happening.

Peter's grandfather, though, was somewhat less ordinary. He lived by himself in a splendidly messy cottage with a canary in a cage and two rabbits in a hutch in the garden.

When Peter went to stay with him they did whatever they both felt like and had french fries with every meal. Sometimes they stayed in bed till lunchtime, and other days they played card games all day, and once they decided to make a five-foot model airplane and sat up all night doing it. I have to tell you that it all came apart the next day, but they both felt it had been worth it.

"Don't forget to buy Grandpa a card for his birthday," Peter's mother had said. The day before the birthday, though, Peter decided that just a card would not do for such an excellent

grandfather. He went off by himself
into the town to look for a present—a
rather special present, it would have
to be.

Tobacco? No, that was boring.
Chocolates? A corkscrew with a handle
in the shape of an anchor? An ashtray
with a map of Cornwall on it? Nothing
he saw seemed right at all. He wandered
into the town square. It was market day

and there were fruit and vegetable stalls
and shirt and jeans stalls and stalls selling
dog food and bird seed, and a great many
people. There was also a junk stall at
which Peter stopped. This was more
promising. He thought about buying a
ship in a green glass bottle, but it was

much more than he could afford. An old
windup gramophone would have been
just the thing, but that was expensive
too.

Then he caught sight of one of those
glass domes on a stand that usually have
a couple of stuffed birds on a branch
under them. This one, though, had a
twiggy nest instead, and inside the nest
were two large reddish speckled eggs.

As soon as Peter saw it he knew that
this would be the perfect present. It
might not be what Grandpa had always
wanted, but he would want it as soon as

he saw it. And it was not too expensive; the glass was cracked and there were several chips out of the stand, so that it had been reduced to two dollars.

Peter bought it.

He was absolutely right—Grandpa was delighted. "Now that's what I call a present," he said. "Original. Not your run-of-the-mill box of handkerchiefs or package of pipe cleaners. Just the thing for my mantelpiece."

So the glass dome was put in the center

of the mantelpiece, and that evening, since it was rather chilly, Grandpa lit a fire and he and Peter sat in front of it and ate hamburgers and french fries off their knees and admired Peter's present. "Victorian, it'll be," said Grandpa. "A hundred years old or so, I'd guess."

It was Peter who came down first in the morning. He opened the curtains and had a look at the weather (raining) and then glanced across the room at the glass dome.

Underneath it, something was moving. He stood stock still and stared. Impossible! He moved closer.

The eggs had gone. In their place were two small lizard-like creatures scratching frantically on the glass. For a few moments Peter gazed in amazement. Then he rushed upstairs to call Grandpa.

Together they inspected the creatures more carefully. They were about five inches long. They had greenish scales blotched with red, legs with tiny claws, long tails with ends barbed like an arrow, and very small . . .

"Wings!" said Grandpa, putting on his glasses. "Would you believe it! Wings— no two ways about it!"

The creatures continued to scratch on the glass. "What they look like," said Peter, hardly daring to say it, "is dragons."

Grandpa nodded. "You've put your finger on it. What we've got here, to my mind, is a pair of young dragons. Extraordinary! It must be the heat of the fire that did it. Those eggs must have been laid away in some cold attic all these years. Bring them into the warmth and they hatch. It's a wonderful thing, Nature."

Clearly, they could not leave the dragons where they were. Apart from anything else, there would not be enough air for them under the glass.

Grandpa found an old cardboard box
which they lined with newspaper. Very
carefully they lifted the glass dome from
its base and tipped the creatures into it.

"Question is," said Grandpa, "what do
we feed them?"

This turned out to be a problem. They
tried breadcrumbs, bird food, cat food,
bananas and lettuce, all of which the

12

dragons ignored. They retreated to the
end of the box and sat there forlornly. It
wasn't until Grandpa and Peter had their
lunch, which was fishsticks and french
fries, that they perked up. They began to
sniff and scratch at the sides of the box.
Peter chopped up a piece of fishstick and
offered it to the dragons. They fell on it
happily.

The dragons flourished. After a week
or so they were getting too big for the

box. Grandpa repaired an old rabbit hutch and they moved them out into the garden and put them in that. They ate a package of fishsticks every day, with a can of salmon as an occasional treat. Nothing else would they touch, except shrimp, which they ate whole, shells and all.

Peter and Grandpa were extremely proud of them. "You can keep your parakeets and your cats and dogs," said Grandpa. "I like an unusual pet. And these beat everything, don't they?"

The dragons, admittedly, were not especially cozy pets. They did not care

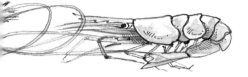

for being stroked and were inclined to
hiss when disturbed. But they were very
handsome. Their scales were now a rich
grass-green decorated with reddish-brown
spots. They had fine crests along their
necks and their tails swished and curled.
Their wings were transparent and large
enough now to flap. They would sit in
their hutch preening and flapping and
nibbling at fishsticks.

Given all this, I suppose what came next was inevitable. Grandpa decided to exhibit the dragons at the town's annual Pet Show.

They attracted immediate attention. And caused instant trouble. "What are they, for heaven's sake?" exclaimed the lady in charge of arranging entries.

"Well," said Grandpa, "you've got a point there. I can see they don't fit in with Dogs or Cats or Birds. Reptiles, maybe?"

Eventually, after a great deal of talk among the judges, the dragons were entered in the Miscellaneous Class, along with some turtles, a tank of frogs, two parrots and a garter snake.

They were a great success. People crowded around their hutch peering through the wire netting at them and exclaiming. The dragons appeared to

enjoy the attention; they strutted up and down and played together. They were now almost the size of rabbits.

The trouble started when it came to the judging. Two of the three judges wanted to give them First Prize but the third objected strongly, on the grounds that nobody knew what to call them. Finally a vote was taken. The dragons

were given a red ribbon, which Grandpa
pinned proudly to the hutch.

The awkward judge, a rather fat woman
whose poodle had failed to win a prize in
the Dog Class, remarked loudly that the
things looked to her like something that
ought to be in a museum and she
wouldn't be surprised if they carried
terrible diseases. She tapped the hutch
with her umbrella and then sprang
backwards with a shriek. There was a
sizzling sound and a smell of scorching.

The dragons had learned to spit
flames. Very small flames, mind you,

but flames all the same. Grandpa and Peter took them home hurriedly, before people could ask any more questions or make any more comments than they already were. On the way Grandpa bought a fire extinguisher.

"Just in case. They were provoked, of course. I think they'll settle down again once we get them home." He spoke severely to the dragons, who looked now as though butter wouldn't melt in their mouths.

There was a short article about them in the newspaper, headed LOCAL RETIREE'S MYSTERY PETS. Grandpa had mixed feelings about this; he thought the photograph of himself unflattering and he was worried that it would arouse too much curiosity.

"There's no limit to how nosy people can be, you take my word for it. Jealous, too. That's what it was with that woman. Plain jealous. Her with her poodle dressed up like a lamb chop. Next thing, we'll have everyone wanting what we've got. And I'm not breeding them. I've had enough trouble that way with rabbits."

He was right to be worried, as it turned out. Three days later there was a knock at the door and on the step stood a man in uniform who said he was the Pest Control Officer and he had reason to believe that there were some unusual animals in the house. Grandpa and Peter stared at him in alarm.

"Lizards of some sort, are they?" continued the Pest Control Officer. "The name's George, by the way." He held out a printed card to Grandpa. "Mr. George. Won't take a minute, but it's my job to

check up. All right if I come in?"

They let him in and took him through to the garden. There was nothing else, really, they could do. Mr. George squatted down in front of the hutch and studied the dragons. There was a silence.

"Ah," said Mr. George. "Yes. I see. A pair of . . . um . . . A pair of those things."

There was a glint, now, in Grandpa's eye. "What," he said, "counts as pests?"

Mr. George stood up. "Rats. Mice.

Cockroaches. Black beetles. Wasps."

"And are what we've got in that hutch any of those?" continued Grandpa.

"Strictly speaking," said Mr. George, "no."

"Then," said Grandpa triumphantly, "what's wrong with us keeping them?'

Mr. George considered. "Strictly speaking," he said again, "nothing." He cast a doubtful look down at the dragons. "But they're a bit unusual, you must admit. What . . . um . . . what exactly would you call them?"

"Dragons," said Peter, before he could help himself.

Mr. George laughed. He patted Peter on the head. "Got quite an imagination, your grandson, hasn't he?" he said to Grandpa. "Well, we'll leave it at that for now. But I'll have to make a report on it. And be sure you keep them under control—they look to me as though they could take a bite out of you."

As soon as he had gone Peter and Grandpa heaved sighs of relief. It had been a dangerous moment, they agreed. "Someone's been tattling," said Grandpa darkly. "Her with her poodle, I daresay. Or one of the busybodies on this street. Best thing we can do is lie low or else . . ."

"Or else we might not be able to keep them?" asked Peter anxiously.

Grandpa nodded.

But there was worse to come. A couple of days later Peter went out in the

evening to feed the dragons and found to
his horror that the hutch was empty.
Part of the wire netting front had been

ripped away, evidently by strong little
dragon claws. He and Grandpa searched
the garden; there was no sign of them.
They remembered with alarm that lately
the dragons had been flapping their
wings more and more, like baby birds
about to take off. Had they flown right

away? Grandpa shook his head sadly. "I don't know how they'd fend for themselves in that case. How're they going to get across to folks that what they like is fishsticks and nothing else?"

"Or canned salmon," added Peter.

They searched the house, just in case, and then came outside again. And then, both at once, they noticed a curious noise coming from the next door garden. A sound of splashing.

"What's Mrs. Hammond up to?" said Grandpa, frowning. Mrs. Hammond was the next-door neighbor.

"But she's away!" Peter exclaimed. "Don't you remember—she asked us to water her tomatoes for her."

They dashed to the fence and looked over. In the middle of Mrs. Hammond's garden was her most treasured possession, a large pond covered with water lilies and bullrushes among which swam several fat goldfish.

And there at the edge of the pond was one of the dragons, contentedly munching a goldfish that it held in its

front claws. Even as they watched, the
second one rose from a clump of rushes,
whooshed up into the air with a noisy

flapping of wings and plunged straight
down into the pond. A few second later
it rose to the surface, scrambled out,

shook itself like a dog and settled down to eat the goldfish that it, too was now clutching.

"She's going to be *furious*!" cried Peter.

Grandpa was already rushing into the house. He came out with a piece of green nylon garden netting and a bucket. "Quick! Over that fence!"

Peter scrambled over and began the difficult business of catching the dragons. Grandpa watched anxiously from the other side and shouted words of advice. The dragons scuttled around the pond hissing angrily and sometimes spitting a few feeble flames. From time to time they took off and flapped a few yards across Mrs. Hammond's lawn before flopping to the ground. Evidently they weren't very good yet at flying. At last Peter managed to net them both and get them into the bucket, which he passed over the fence to Grandpa. There were only three goldfish left in the pond.

They put the dragons back in the hutch, where they huddled in the corner still hissing quietly. Peter and Grandpa hurried off to the pet store on

High Street and they bought the
entire stock of goldfish.

"Think she'll notice the difference?"
asked Peter when he had emptied them
into Mrs. Hammond's pond.

Grandpa shook his head. "I doubt if a person gets what you might call close to a fish."

That evening they took a long hard look at the situation. Things could not go on like this.

"You know something?" said Grandpa. "I think I know what it is we've got out there. What we've got is a pair of sea-dragons. Fish-eaters, see? I should have caught on to it before."

"Do you think they're full size yet?" asked Peter.

Grandpa shrugged. "Maybe, maybe not. But one thing I'm clear about; they're getting out of hand. They're not the sort of thing you can keep in your backyard forever."

The more they thought about it the more it seemed to them that there were only two things they could do. They

could give the dragons to a zoo. Or they could let them go.

"They'd hate it in a zoo," said Peter. "Being stared at all the time. And fed peanuts. But where could we let them go?"

"Where they ought to be," said Grandpa. "Their natural habitat. The sea."

And so the great idea was born. It took a lot of planning. They would have to take the dragons to the coast on the bus, since Grandpa did not have a car. Then they would have to find a beach with rocky cliffs from which to launch the dragons.

They borrowed a cat carrier from a
neighbor (Grandpa told a story about
having to take his rabbits to the vet), got
the dragons into it, with some difficulty,
and set off. The bus trip was tricky;
the dragons scratched around in the
basket throughout the trip so that
Grandpa and Peter had to talk loudly to
drown the noise. But at last they reached
the coast and set off for a beach where
Grandpa knew there were cliffs dropping
down into the sea.

There were a good number of people on the beach at the foot of the cliffs. Grandpa and Peter stood at the top of the path that led down there and watched for a few minutes.

"Be all right so long as we can get them off good and quick," said Grandpa. "Straight out to sea and no nonsense."

They opened the cat basket. Peter pushed it nearer to the edge of the cliff. The dragons stuck their heads out and flapped their wings. They climbed onto the edge of the basket and flapped more busily.

"That's it," said Peter. "Shoo! Go on— fly!"

And the dragons took off. They soared
upward and then . . . oh, horrors! . . .
they began to sink slowly toward the
beach. They spun and flapped and
fluttered down at last upon the sand.
Peter and Grandpa gave one look, and set
off at once helter-skelter down the steep
path to the beach.

They got to the spot at which the
dragons had landed and began to search
for them. People were sitting around
having picnics or sunbathing or reading
newspapers. There was no sign of the
dragons. Suddenly Peter caught sight of

one of them. It was sitting beside
someone's picnic basket contentedly
munching a tuna fish sandwich. And the
other one was stretched out on the
top of some children's sandcastle,
sunning itself.

Peter rushed forward to grab them at the same moment as the owner of the tuna fish sandwich turned around and gave a cry of alarm.

"Excuse me!" Peter panted. "My dog . . . " He snatched up the dragon just as the man was reaching for his glasses. He seized the other one and popped them both into the cat carrier, which Grandpa was holding out.

Several people were now staring at them and muttering. They made for the cliff path, hastily.

At the top Grandpa said grimly, "One more try. Or it's the zoo for the pair of them. We've done our level best."

A breeze had sprung up. Perhaps that helped, or perhaps the dragons had simply gotten better at flying after a little practice. Anyway, this time they soared upward and stayed up, floating and flapping over the beach and the people and out over the water. "That's the spirit!" cried Grandpa. Peter clapped and waved.

The dragons whisked their tails and swooped in circles. Their scales caught the sun and glittered until after a few minutes all Peter and Grandpa could see was two twinkling spots of light. And as they watch the two spots plunged down suddenly into the sea, and then sprang up out of it again in a gleaming shower, then down and up again . . .

"They're fishing!" cried Peter. And he and Grandpa turned away and began to walk slowly back to the road to catch the bus.

Maybe those were the last dragons in Cornwall. Maybe not. There's no telling. As Grandpa said, it's a wonderful thing, Nature.